THE HONEYBEE

Kirsten Hall   Isabelle Arsenault

ATHENEUM
BOOKS FOR YOUNG READERS
New York   London   Toronto   Sydney   New Delhi

A field.
A tree.
Climb it and see...

For miles, all around you,
grow wild and free

FLOWERS.

But then...
Shhh!
What's that?

Do you hear it?

You're near it.

It's closer,
it's coming,
it's buzzing,
it's humming....

Four tiny wings;
they buzz and they sing.
They're clapping and flapping;
the busy bee's lapping.

LAP,
LAP,
LAP,

TAP,
TAP,
TAP,

searching,
perching...

THIS ONE.

This is the flower the bee has chosen.
This is the flower the pollen grows in.
This is the flower, its color so bright,
its sweet blooming scent calls the bee from its flight.

Such a long trip,
it's time for a sip,
SUGARY,
WATERY...

NECTAR.

There now, it drills now,
the bee sips and spills now,

there now, it swills now,
it sits oh-so-still now.

There now, it fills now,

it's back to the hill now....

More pollen,
more nectar—
it's mealtime,
BUZZ, BUZZ!

BUZZ, BUZZ, a crowd.
Swarming and teeming and loud.

Flapping,
flying,
landing,
prying.

ALL OF THIS NECTAR,
IT'S OURS!
IT'S OURS!

They work on the flowers
for hours and hours.
Until...

little bees with heavy sacs,

lifting,
  shifting,
    turning back.

ZOOM, they race!
ZOOM, they chase!
ZOOM, they zoom
and pick up the pace.
And then

ZOOOOOOOOOOOOM!

They see it up ahead....

OUR HIVE!
OUR HIVE!
OUR HIDING PLACE!

Watch them arrive,
watch how their hive
buzzes alive—

BUZZ!

A dance begins.
Waggle,
wiggle.

The dance is lovely.
Tremble,
jiggle.

The dance goes straight now—in a line—
a figure eight is the final sign.

OH! NOW WE KNOW!

WE KNOW WHERE TO GO!

THANKS FOR THE SECRETS!

(AND THANKS FOR THE SHOW!)

New foragers leave
on a searching mission . . .

while house bees march forward
with hungry ambition!

CHEW, CHEW — THAT'S WHAT WE DO,

WE SUCK OUT THE NECTAR,
WE SUCK IT STRAIGHT THROUGH.

CHEW, CHEW — WE'RE CHANGING ITS MAKEUP,
WE'RE GIVING THE NECTAR A CHEMICAL SHAKE-UP.

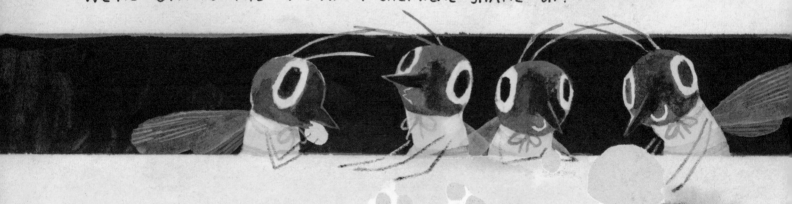

CHEW, CHEW — WE MAKE IT LIKE GLUE.

MAKE IT THICK, MAKE IT STICK,
MAKE IT SLICK, MAKE IT NEW!

CHEW, CHEW, CHEW, CHEW —
AT LAST, WE'RE FINALLY THROUGH.

But there's more to do at home...

... like fill
the honeycomb!
They jam its cells
with nectar-plaster,
then rev up their engines
and beat their
wings faster....

WHOOSH!
They're strong
despite their size.

SWOOSH!
The nectar cools
and dries.

It's getting thicker now....
Wings move quicker now....

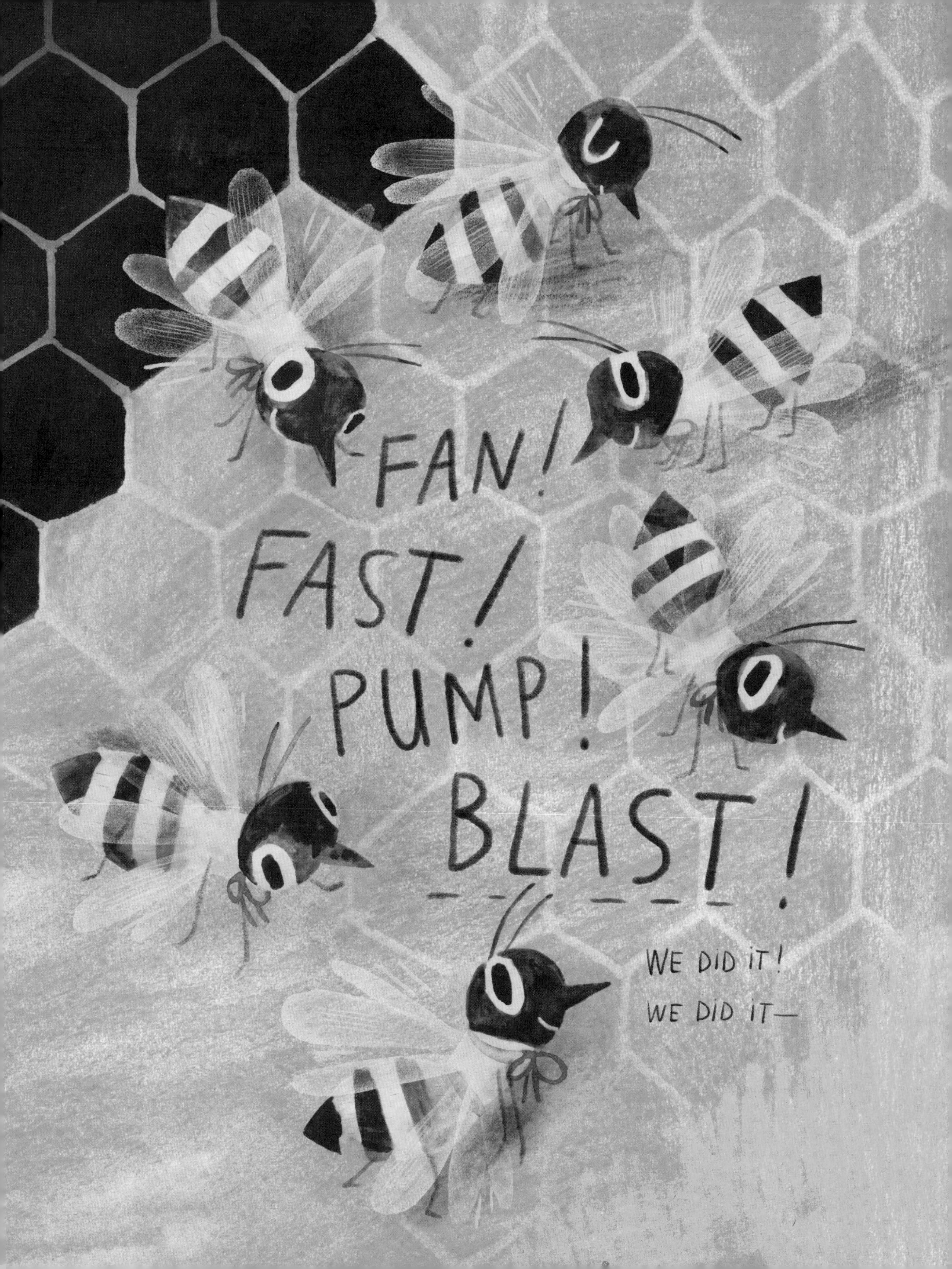
FAN!
FAST!
PUMP!
BLAST!
WE DID IT!
WE DID IT—

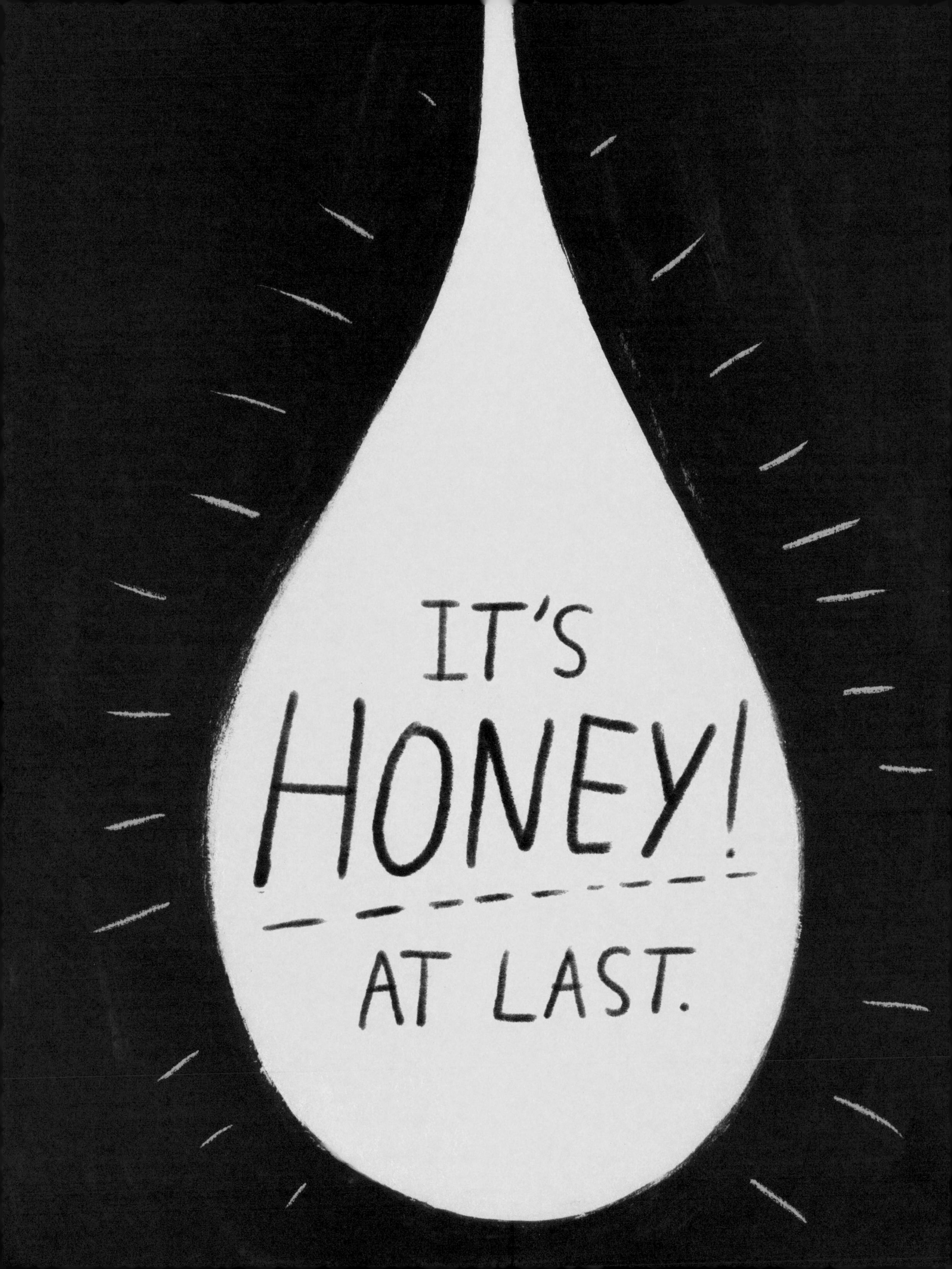
IT'S
HONEY!
AT LAST.

And now,
to keep it
safe....

Tiny honey cells
are capped.
Liquid gold is sealed
and trapped.

And only when
it's needed most—
a hungry day—
will these vaults
be tapped.

Outside the hive come shorter days.
Cooler winds and softer rays,
fewer eggs to birth and raise....

With the queen less busy,
the hive's less buzzy,
and bees amass
all soft and fuzzy.

POP!
A bud.

DRIP!
Some mud.

Creatures stir in the melting snow,
    and inside the hive, the bees—
        they know.

HUM! It's springtime!
HUM! Life anew!

One little bee in a tree
knows what to do.

Watch it
ZOOOOOOOOOM!

A field.
A tree.
Climb it and see...

From a faraway hive
flew this hardworking,
honey-sweet…

BEE.

Dear Reader,

I wrote this story for an important reason. The honeybee is one of our world's most marvelous creatures. And sadly, it's in danger. In writing this book, I was hoping you might grow a new appreciation for the honeybee—and that you'll join me in caring about its future.

HONEYBEES ARE BEEAUTIFUL CREATURES.

They're just like us! They live in families (called colonies) and in homes (called hives). They work hard. Each bears on its tiny back a big responsibility toward the larger unit. Honeybees hum, they buzz, they zoom, they sip, they dance, and they even nestle. And while we shouldn't get too close to honeybees—they can sting!—I wanted you to have an up close look at all the wonderful things they do.

WHAT WOULD THE WORLD BEE WITHOUT HONEYBEES ?

Without honeybees, we'd be in trouble! Honeybees fly from plant to plant, hunting for and sipping nectar. While they travel, they spread pollen. The pollen they spread causes seeds to form. And the new seeds lead to new plants. We rely heavily on these plants for our food, clothing, and shelter.

HOW CAN YOU BEE HELPFUL TO THE HONEYBEE ?

Here are five simple ways you can help the honeybee survive:

1. PLANT FLOWERS AND HERBS WHEREVER YOU CAN.

And try to plant lots of the same types together. (Bees like that!) Some of the honeybee's favorite plants are lavender, lilacs, mint, poppies, pumpkins, rosemary, sage, squash, sunflowers, and tomatoes. Avoid using chemicals and pesticides on your plants. They're dangerous to the honeybee and are linked to its decline.

2. WELCOME WEEDS AND WILD PLANTS !

It's easy to want to get rid of weeds! Some people think leaving weeds unpicked means you haven't tidied up enough. But honeybees love them. Weeds can be havens for honeybees, and wildflowers are one of their most important sources of food.

3. BUY HONEY — FROM A LOCAL BEEKEEPER.

Honey is available at most farmers' markets and stores that carry products from your area's beekeepers. And honey is packed with nutrients. Bake with it! Steep tea with it! Eat a spoonful of it! (But don't have too much at one time; it's delicious but quite sugary!) When you support beekeepers, you keep bees "in business."

4. DON'T BEE AFRAID OF BEES !

Honeybees want nectar and pollen—not to sting or harm you. When bees fly near, stay still. And stay calm, too! Bees can actually "smell" fear. If you stay still and calm, chances are the bee will quickly decide to just fly away. Also, avoid going near beehives. Bees are territorial. But as long as you stay out of their way, they'll stay out of yours.

5. TELL CONGRESS YOU LOVE BEES !

The people who make laws about what we can and can't do need to work harder to protect the honeybee. When our laws don't protect our environment, honeybees are in danger. Write a letter to your local politicians. Tell them you love bees, and why they're important! Draw pictures and use your voice. If enough of us work together, maybe we can save the future of the honeybee.

Thanks for caring. And BEE proud of yourself! You know so much now about the honeybee, and information is power. Let's go BEE powerful advocates for the honeybee together!

Love,
Kirsten

This book is for all of you who love
and cherish our world's beautiful and endangered creatures.

With special thanks to Ann Bobco and Emma Ledbetter

—K. H. and I. A.

ATHENEUM BOOKS FOR YOUNG READERS
An imprint of Simon & Schuster Children's Publishing Division
1230 Avenue of the Americas, New York, New York 10020
Text copyright © 2018 by Kirsten Hall
Illustrations copyright © 2018 by Isabelle Arsenault
All rights reserved, including the right of reproduction in whole or in part in any form.
ATHENEUM BOOKS FOR YOUNG READERS is a registered trademark of Simon & Schuster, Inc.
Atheneum logo is a trademark of Simon & Schuster, Inc.
For information about special discounts for bulk purchases, please contact
Simon & Schuster Special Sales at 1-866-506-1949 or business@simonandschuster.com.
The Simon & Schuster Speakers Bureau can bring authors to your live event. For more information or to book an event,
contact the Simon & Schuster Speakers Bureau at 1-866-248-3049 or visit our website at www.simonspeakers.com.
Book design by Ann Bobco and Isabelle Arsenault
The text for this book was set in a font named Honeybee that was designed by Isabelle Arsenault.
The illustrations for this book were rendered using ink, gouache, pencil, and colored pencil.
Manufactured in China — 0218 SCP — First Edition
2 4 6 8 10 9 7 5 3 1
Library of Congress Cataloging-in-Publication Data
Names: Hall, Kirsten, author. | Arsenault, Isabelle, 1978– illustrator.
Title: The honeybee / by Kirsten Hall ; illustrated by Isabelle Arsenault.
Description: First edition. | New York : Atheneum Books for Young Readers, [2018] |
Summary: Illustrations and rhyming text follow endangered honeybees through the year
as they forage for pollen and nectar, communicate with others at their hive, and make honey.
Identifiers: LCCN 2017000369 | ISBN 9781481469975 (hardcover) | ISBN 9781481469982 (eBook)
Subjects: | CYAC: Stories in rhyme. | Honeybee—Fiction.
Classification: LCC PZ8.3.H146 Hon 2018 | DDC [E]—dc23
LC record available at https://lccn.loc.gov/2017000369